DINOSAURS
FOR LUNCH

SHELLY RITTHALER lives with her husband and daughter on a ranch in Wyoming. Shelly enjoys walking, bird watching and collecting wildflowers. She loves reading, movies, animals and dinosaurs.

DINOSAURS FOR LUNCH

SHELLY RITTHALER

Illustrated by Gioia Fiammenghi

AN AVON  CAMELOT BOOK

To Reuben and Min Dee
Thanks for your support, inspiration and love

DINOSAURS FOR LUNCH is an original publication of Avon Books. This work has never before appeared in book form.

AVON BOOKS
A division of
The Hearst Corporation
1350 Avenue of the Americas
New York, New York 10019

Text copyright © 1993 by Shelly Ritthaler
Illustrations copyright © 1993 by Avon Books
Illustrations by Gioia Fiammenghi
Published by arrangement with the author
Library of Congress Catalog Card Number: 93-90399
ISBN: 0-380-76796-1
RL: 2.7

First Avon Camelot Printing: December 1993

CAMELOT TRADEMARK REG. U.S. PAT. OFF. AND IN OTHER COUNTRIES, MARCA REGISTRADA, HECHO EN U.S.A.

Printed in the U.S.A.

OPM   10 9 8 7 6 5 4 3 2 1

CONTENTS

CHAPTER ONE

Rules

The rules said, *Don't Push*. Every second grader at Wilson Elementary School knew the rules. But Kevin Jackson didn't care about rules. He waited until the teacher wasn't looking and pushed anyway.

Danny Clark knew the rules. He quietly stood in line waiting to go into the school building after morning recess. When Kevin pushed him, he didn't know what happened. He felt a heavy shove in his back and he fell forward. His chin smacked the sidewalk. His hands skidded in the gravel. He couldn't get his breath. Blood trickled from the cut on his chin.

"Have a nice trip?" Kevin said with a mean smile and a laugh.

Min Dee Ritter stepped out of the other line and reached down to help Danny. "Are you okay?" she asked.

Danny tried not to cry. But he couldn't help it.

"Min Dee Ritter, get in line!" said Mrs. Dummitt, the playground teacher. Her sharp voice made all of the second graders, except Min Dee, scurry into their places.

"Kevin pushed Danny," Min Dee said to Mrs. Dummitt.

"Min Dee, get in line," Mrs. Dummitt snapped.

"He did it on purpose," Min Dee said as she stood between the two lines of students.

"That will be enough, Min Dee," Mrs. Dummitt said with a stern look in her eye.

"I saw it. You're not supposed to push,

but Kevin pushed Danny.'' Min Dee's chin pointed up at the teacher. Her short, black hair glistened in the sun.

"Min Dee, you will report to the principal's office after school. You will sit on the naughty bench for one half-hour tonight. Maybe that will teach you not to talk back to a teacher.''

Min Dee stepped into the line with a pout. "It's not fair,'' she whispered.

Mrs. Dummitt heard her. She pointed her finger at Min Dee and ordered, *"Enough."* Then she turned and led the two lines of second graders into the school. Danny rubbed the blood off of his chin with the back of his hand. Kevin snickered. "What's a matter, Danny,'' he said. "Have to have a girl to protect you?''

CHAPTER TWO

Bumps, Scrapes, and Bruises

Danny's chin didn't quit bleeding. His teacher, Miss Martin, sent him to the nurse's office. The nurse bandaged it and told him not to play so rough. Danny tried to tell her he wasn't playing when it happened. He was standing in line when Kevin pushed him. The nurse shook her head. Then she bustled away to take care of another student.

The bleeding stopped by the time noon recess came. Danny walked out on the playground. He didn't feel good. His chin throbbed. The scratches on his hands ached, and his knees felt bruised. He touched the bandage on his chin as he watched the other boys running across the playground. He didn't feel like running. He noticed Min Dee sitting by herself on a swing. He went over and sat in an empty swing beside her. "Hi," he said.

"Hi, Danny," she said in a miserable voice. "How is your chin?"

"It's okay. I went to the nurse. I'm sorry you have to stay after school. Will your mom be mad?"

Min Dee shrugged. "She says I talk back too much. I'll probably get in trouble. Kevin Jackson is the meanest boy in this school. I hate him. I don't know why Mrs. Dummitt doesn't do something to him. Look at him over by the monkey bars."

They looked across the playground and saw Kevin pulling on Erica Bradley's long, blonde braids. Mrs. Dummitt was standing in the corner of the playground with her back to the school. She pulled a paperback book out of her big, sweater pocket. She hid it in the crook of her arm and began secretly reading.

"She's supposed to be watching the playground, not reading," Danny said. "She doesn't care if Kevin hurts somebody."

They quietly watched as Erica Bradley jerked her braids away from Kevin. She ran over to Mrs. Dummitt. Min Dee said, "She's telling on him. I bet he doesn't get into trouble." Danny nodded. They watched Mrs. Dummitt point toward the swings and shake her finger at Erica.

Erica slowly walked to the swings and sat in the empty one beside Danny. She wiped a tear off her cheek. "Did Kevin hurt you?" Min Dee asked.

"Yes," Erica sniffed. "I told Mrs. Dummitt. She told me to quit being a tattletale. Kevin wants me to give him my allowance money. He said he would leave me alone if I do."

"You should tell your mom," Danny told her.

7

"No," she said. "Kevin said he would beat me up if I told my parents. They give me lots of money. I'll just ask my mom to give me more. Besides, I'm having a birthday party. And I'm inviting everyone in both second grade classes, except for Kevin. It's going to be the biggest, best birthday party ever. We're going to have pizza, ice cream, and cake. And my mom is going to hire a clown to do magic tricks. And I'm not inviting Kevin. So there." She held her nose in the air, sniffed and strutted away to play with a group of girls.

As Danny watched her, he said, "I have to make my bed and take out the trash and do the dishes or I don't get my allowance. My mom won't give me more money. I'm not going to give him my money."

"I don't get an allowance," Min Dee said. "My mom gives me money some- times. But I have to tell her what I want to buy. She won't let me buy junk. I know she won't give me money to give to

8

Kevin. And even if I did have some money, I wouldn't give it to him." She kicked at the gravel in front of her. That's when Danny noticed her shoes. They were high-top sneakers with red, yellow, blue, and green dinosaurs all over them.

"I like your shoes. Where did you get them?" he asked. "I love dinosaurs."

Min Dee held her feet up so Danny could look at her shoes. "My mom bought them. I don't know where. I'll ask her."

"I have a dinosaur collection," he told her. "I'm going to ask my mom to get me a pair of dinosaur shoes."

A voice rang out behind them. They turned to see Kevin standing behind them pointing a finger and singing: "Two little lovebirds sitting on the swings. K-I-S-S-I-N-G. First comes love, then comes marriage, then comes Min Dee with a baby carriage."

Kevin and the other boys with him laughed and ran away. The bell rang for the students to line up and go into the building.

"You should slug him," Min Dee said as she slid out of the swing. "You're bigger than he is."

They quietly walked to the ends of the lines. Danny took his place. Min Dee lined up with the rest of her class. Toward the front of the line, Kevin was poking one of the other children in the back. He stopped and stood quietly when Mrs. Dummitt walked between the two lines. She looked to see if everyone was ready to go into the building. Her book stuck out of the top of her sweater pocket. She walked back to the front of the lines. When her back was turned, Min Dee looked at Danny. She curled up her fist and shook it at Kevin. "You should pop him," she whispered to Danny.

Danny looked down at the ground and kicked a piece of gravel off the sidewalk. He knew it was against the rules to hit.

CHAPTER THREE

Girls Calling

That night, after school, Danny's mom washed the cuts on his hands and chin. She made him pull down his jeans. She looked at the bruises on his knees. As she stuck clean bandages on the scrapes, she said, "Kevin sounds like a nasty boy."

"He is," Danny said.

"Is he just mean to you or is he mean to other children, too?" his mom asked.

"He's mean to everybody. He told Erica to give him some money. He told

her he would leave her alone if she did,"
Danny told her.

"You didn't give him any money, did
you?" Mom asked with a stern look in
her eye.

"No," Danny said.

"Don't you give him any money," she
said. "If he tries to push you or hurt you
again, tell the playground teacher."

"I did tell her," Danny said as she put
the box of bandages in the cupboard.
"She won't do anything about him."

"I have trouble believing that," Mom
said. "Tell you what, the best thing you
can do is stay away from Kevin. Just stay
as far away as you can. If he comes where
you are playing, you go somewhere else
to play. Stay away from him."

Danny tried to tell her that Mrs. Dummitt wouldn't listen, but his baby sister
started to cry. The phone rang.

Mom rushed out of the bathroom. "Just
stay away from Kevin and things will be
fine," she said as she left.

"Danny," Mike yelled, "telephone."

13

Danny pulled up his pants and went to the kitchen. His mom held his baby sister and stirred the potatoes cooking on the stove. Mike, Danny's sixth-grade brother, held his hand over the telephone receiver. "Danny," he whispered. "Telephone for you. It's a girl." Mike snickered and sang, "Danny has a girlfriend. Danny has a girlfriend." Mike puckered his lips as he handed the phone to Danny. "Kissy face. Kissy face."

Danny scowled at his older brother. He placed the phone over his ear and said, "Hello." He tried to turn so that the others couldn't hear him talking.

"Hi, Danny, this is Min Dee," she said.

"Hi, Min Dee. Did you get in trouble for having to stay after school?" he asked.

"A little bit. I have to do the dishes for a week. It's not so bad."

"Gee, I'm sorry," Danny said. "I tried to tell my mom about Kevin. She won't listen. She said to stay away from him."

Min Dee sighed. "That's not so easy

to do. I think he likes to follow people around and pick on them. Hey, guess what? I asked my mom where she got my dinosaur shoes. She said, Carlson's Department Store. Maybe your mom will get you some. Can I come over to your house to play tomorrow after school? My mom said I could.''

''I'll have to ask,'' Danny told her. He pulled the telephone away from his ear, held it close to his chest, and said, ''Mom, can Min Dee come over and play after school tomorrow?''

''Woo-woo. Having your girlfriend over?'' Mike said with a snort and a giggle. ''Sounds pretty serious.''

''Mike, hush,'' Mom said as she set plates on the table. ''I suppose it will be all right, Danny.''

Danny stuck out his tongue at Mike. It was against the family rules to listen to other people's telephone calls. He wished Mike would go in the other room. Danny put the telephone back to his ear. ''You can come over, Min Dee.'' Mike started

to laugh and tease Danny. "Min Dee, I have to go now," Danny told her. "Bye, I'll see you tomorrow." He hung up the telephone. Mike wrestled Danny to the floor and pretended to kiss him. Danny screamed, "Mike, stop it! Cut it out!" Mike wouldn't quit. Danny made a fist and tried to hit him.

In a stern voice, Mom said, "That will be enough. We don't hit each other, and we don't wrestle in the kitchen. Mike, no more teasing. Do you boys have your homework done?" The boys pulled away from each other. "Go wash for supper," she ordered.

That night at the supper table, Danny's dad asked him about the bandage on his chin. "Kevin Jackson pushed me," Danny told him.

"Hmm," Dad said as he took another bite of mashed potatoes. "Sounds like someone to stay away from."

"Guess what, Dad?" Mike said. "Danny has a girlfriend. She's coming over tomorrow after school."

"I do not have a girlfriend," Danny said.

"If she's not your girlfriend, what is she?" Mike asked.

"Boys, that will be enough," Mom said. "Be nice to each other, or you can go to your rooms."

"Mom?" Danny asked. "Can I have a pair of dinosaur shoes?"

"What are dinosaur shoes?" Mom asked.

"They're sneakers with dinosaurs on them. We can buy them at Carlson's Department Store."

"Where did you see them?" Mom asked.

"Min Dee has a pair," Danny said.

"Ha, ha," Mike shouted with glee. "I told you Danny has a girlfriend. Now he wants to dress like her."

"I do not," Danny shouted. "I just want some dinosaur shoes. There's nothing wrong with that."

"You want them because your girlfriend has some," Mike said.

"That is enough," Mom said. "You boys stop fighting. Mike, I don't want to hear another word out of you. Do you understand? Leave Danny alone."

The family quietly finished eating supper. Afterward, Danny helped his mom clean the table. He stacked the dirty dishes beside the sink for her. She washed the dishes. When they were alone in the kitchen, Danny said, "Guess what, Mom? Miss Martin has a friend who digs up dinosaur bones. She told us about him today. He digs up the bones and cleans them so he can put them in the museum. We might take a field trip to go to the place where he works. Miss Martin called it a dig. She's going to ask the principal if our class can go to the dig."

"That sounds like fun," Mom said. "You'll really love that, won't you?"

"Yeah. Miss Martin said not to get excited about it until she finds out if we can go. I sure hope we can." Danny took a deep breath. "Mom? Can I have a pair of dinosaur shoes?"

"I don't think so, Danny. You have a perfectly good pair of sneakers. I know you love dinosaurs, but we'll just have to wait until your shoes wear out before we get another pair."

Danny nodded as he left the kitchen. He went to his room and sat on his bed. The shelves in Danny's room were lined with dinosaurs of every size, kind, and color. He had dinosaurs made of metal, plastic, and paper. He even had one very, very special one. It was made of glass. Danny stood on his bed and took his special glass dinosaur from the shelf. He cradled it in his hands as he sat down again.

His grandmother had been on a vacation. She went to a place where people called glass blowers work. They made the dinosaur out of thin glass rods that they melted in a fire. While the glass was melted, they formed it into all kinds of figures and shapes. Grandma asked them to make a dinosaur for Danny. She gave it to him when she came home from her vacation.

Danny always treated the dinosaur carefully. Grandma had told him it could break very easily. Danny ran his fingers over the tiny glass dinosaur. Then he had a great idea. He thought of a way to get a pair of dinosaur shoes.

CHAPTER FOUR

Ask Grandma

Danny set the dinosaur back on the shelf and went to the living room to talk to his mother. "Mom, do you care if I call Grandma?"

"What do you want to call Grandma for?" she asked.

"I just wanted to see how she is," Danny said as he looked at the floor.

Mom studied Danny before she spoke. "You aren't going to ask Grandma to buy those shoes, are you?"

Danny fidgeted. That was his plan.

Grandma almost never said no to anything. "Not exactly," Danny said slowly. "I was going to see if she had some odd jobs I could do for her so I could earn some money to buy them myself."

Mom sighed. "I suppose that's okay. But you must do something to earn the money. I don't want Grandma to just give them to you. Grandma doesn't have a lot of money to just give it away all the time. Do you understand?"

"Yes," Danny answered. He went to the kitchen phone and dialed his Grandmother's number. "Hi, Grandma," he said when he heard her cheery hello.

"Why, Danny, sweetheart. How are you, dear?"

"I'm fine, Grandma. Grandma, do you have some odd jobs you need done?"

"Well I don't know, sweetheart. Is there something you wanted?"

"Sort of. I have a friend who has a pair of dinosaur shoes. Her Mom bought them at Carlson's Department Store. I want a pair, too. Real bad."

"Oh?" she said sweetly. "Would you like Grandma to get you a pair?"

"I need to earn the money to buy them myself," Danny told her. "I thought if you had some odd jobs, I could do them for you."

"I don't know why your mother won't let me buy you a little something now and then if I want to," Grandma said.

"I don't know why not either, Grandma. It's one of her rules," Danny sighed.

"I know, I know," Grandma said. "Tell you what, sweetheart, you come over tomorrow after school, and I'll have a couple of little jobs for you. Okay? We'll see if we can't get you a pair of dinosaur shoes. How's that?"

"Thanks, Grandma. I love you."

"I love you, sweetie. I'll see you tomorrow."

Danny hung up the phone and went back in the living room. His mom gently rocked the baby. His dad sat in his easy chair reading the paper. Mike sat on the floor playing with a model airplane. "Mom?" Danny said. "Grandma told me to come over tomorrow after school, and she would have a job for me. Is that okay?"

"That's fine, Danny," Mom said.

"Oh, yeah?" Mike said. "What are you going to do about your girlfriend? She's supposed to come over tomorrow."

Danny had forgotten about Min Dee. "What should I do?" he asked his mom.

"It's up to you, Danny. You better call her. Maybe she would like to go over to Grandma's with you. Or, you can ask her to come over another day. Ask her what she wants to do. Grandma would probably like to meet her."

"Yes," Mike said. "It's so important for the girlfriend to meet the family."

"Shut up, Mike," Danny shouted.

"Boys, enough," Mom warned. "You're going to wake the baby. I'm getting sick and tired of this fighting. Mike, stop teasing Danny. Do you understand?" Mike nodded. When Mom turned to look at the baby, Mike smirked at Danny.

Danny went to the kitchen. He found Min Dee's phone number in the book. He dialed and waited. Min Dee answered. "Hi, Min Dee," he said. "I have to go over to help my grandma tomorrow after school, so I can't play. Do you want to come with me or play another day?"

"Where does your grandma live?" she asked.

"A few blocks from my house," Danny told her.

"What do you have to do for her?" Min Dee asked.

"I don't know. I'm going to do some jobs for her. She is going to pay me so I can earn some money to buy some dinosaur shoes like yours."

"Oh, wow," Min Dee squealed. "Hold on." Danny heard the phone clatter. Pretty soon, Min Dee picked up the phone again. "Hey, Danny, my mom said I could go to your grandma's with you. I can help you. Then you'll get done faster."

"Okay, I'll see you tomorrow," Danny said as he hung up the telephone.

He went back to the living room. He told his mom, "Min Dee is going to Grandma's with me."

Mike doubled over with laughter. He rolled around the floor and hooted with giggles. "Danny's in love," he squealed.

Danny turned without speaking. He went to his room and sat on his bed. He wondered if taking Min Dee to his grandma's house was a good idea. He tried to think of a reason to tell her she couldn't go with him. As hard as he tried, he couldn't think of a good reason. He wondered what would happen if he told her they couldn't play together because he didn't want people to think she was his girlfriend.

CHAPTER FIVE

The New Game

The next morning, as Danny walked to school, he decided to tell Min Dee he couldn't play because he had a disease. But then, he couldn't think of the name of a disease.

When he arrived at school, Min Dee was waiting for him at the playground gate. "Guess what," she said with a big smile. "Last night, I thought of a great game we can play. We can play dinosaurs. You can be a meat eater. I'll be a long neck apatosaurus. We can pretend we are

29

in the jungle looking for food. And I'll help you find some food. It'll be lots of fun. What do you think?''

Danny forgot about trying to think of a disease. He forgot about telling her she couldn't play with him. He forgot about telling her she couldn't go to his grandma's house after school. The new game sounded like fun. He wanted to play. He wanted to pretend to be a ferocious, meateating tyrannosaurus rex. He wanted to be the king of the dinosaurs. ''I like your new game,'' he told her. ''Let's play it today.''

They spent the rest of the morning recess planning where to play the new game. They picked a corner of the playground to be their cave. The monkey bars would be the quicksand. They would have to watch out for it. If they got stuck in the quicksand, they would have to save each other. The rest of the playground would be their hunting ground.

They took so much time planning the dinosaur game, they didn't have time to play it. They decided to play it during noon recess.

Danny had fun that morning. He was excited to play the new game.

After lunch, he met Min Dee in the corner of the playground. Min Dee used the heel of her tennis shoe to draw lines in the gravel. "These are the walls of our cave," she said. "And this is the door."

"The door needs to be bigger," Danny told her. "We're big dinosaurs."

Min Dee smiled and drew a bigger door. They ran across the playground looking for dinosaur food. When they returned to their cave, Erica stood in it crying.

"What's wrong?" Min Dee asked.

"Kevin twisted my arm. It hurt. I told Mrs. Dummitt. She said to quit being a tattletale."

Min Dee looked at the red marks on Erica's arm. "I thought you were going to give him some money?" she said.

"I forgot my money today," Erica sniffled. "I'm not inviting him to my

birthday party. My mom is going to buy lots of candy for it. And he can't have any.''

Min Dee looked at Danny. ''Should we let her play dinosaurs with us?'' she asked.

Danny shrugged. ''I don't care.''

''You can play with us,'' Min Dee said. ''This is our cave. You can be our prey. We'll chase you and catch you so we can eat you.''

Erica wiped the tears off her cheek. ''That doesn't sound like fun to me. I'm going to go swing,'' she said with a sniff.

Min Dee sighed. ''Some people just don't know how to have fun. Come on, king of the dinosaurs, let's go.'' They raced across the playground like wild dinosaurs. When they returned, Kevin was standing in the corner of the fence where their cave was supposed to be. He had taken his foot and erased all the lines Min Dee had drawn to mark the walls and the door.

''Hey, who messed up our cave?'' Min Dee asked.

''It was a stupid cave,'' Kevin said.

33

"It was our cave," Min Dee shouted. "You had no right. I'm telling on you."

"Go ahead. Nothing will happen." Kevin snickered.

Out of the corner of his eye, Danny saw Mrs. Dummitt standing against the school building. Her arms were crossed in front of her. He knew she hid a paperback book in her arms. It wouldn't do any good to go tell her.

Min Dee yelled, "Get out of our cave. We were here first."

"You weren't here when I got here," Kevin said as he leaned against the fence.

Danny tugged on Min Dee's sleeve. "Come on Min Dee, we can go play somewhere else."

"If you pay me some money, I'll leave," Kevin said.

Danny pulled on Min Dee's arm and tried to get her to walk away from Kevin. "I don't have any money," Min Dee said. "Danny's grandma is going to give him some . . ." Min Dee covered her mouth with her hand. She wished she hadn't said that.

"Come on, Min Dee, let's go some-where else," Danny whispered.

"You're a pig," Min Dee told Kevin, sticking out her tongue at him. She followed Danny.

"I shouldn't have told him about the money," Min Dee said. "I don't know why I did. It just slipped out."

"It's okay," Danny said.

"I hate him," Min Dee said.

"My mom and dad said to stay away from him," Danny said. "Then there won't be any trouble."

They went to another corner of the playground. They traced new lines in the gravel with their feet for the walls of their new dinosaur cave. They built their new cave bigger and better than their old one.

As Danny drew the door, he had a bad feeling Min Dee was right. He didn't think she should have told Kevin about the money his grandma was going to give him. He worried that it might cause more trouble.

CHAPTER SIX

Grandma's House

The last bell for the day rang. Miss Martin, Danny's teacher, dismissed the class. Danny stuffed his papers into his book bag and tied his sweater around his waist. When he stepped outside the classroom door, Kevin was standing in the hall.

"How much money is your grandma going to give you?" Kevin asked him.

"I don't know," Danny said. "I have to do some jobs, and she is going to pay me." Danny walked toward the outside doors. Kevin followed him.

"Bring it tomorrow and show me how much she gives you," Kevin dared.

"I'm going to save it," Danny told him. "I want to buy some new sneakers."

They reached the doors. Danny pushed on the handle and stepped outside into the sunshine.

"Tell your mom to buy them," Kevin said.

Min Dee stood by the door waiting for Danny. "Shut up, Kevin," she said. "You're a pig."

"Who asked you, China-woman," Kevin said in an ugly voice.

Tears welled up in Min Dee's eyes. "Let's go, Danny," she whispered. She and Danny turned and walked down the sidewalk. Min Dee wiped her eyes with the sleeve of her sweater.

Kevin yelled, "Bring the money tomorrow, Danny. Or you'll be sorry. And don't kiss your China-woman girlfriend."

"Are you okay?" Danny asked when they crossed the street.

"I don't know why people have to be so mean," she said.

"I'm sorry he said all that stuff,"

37

Danny said. "Are you really from China?" Until Kevin had called her China-woman, Danny had never really noticed Min Dee's shiny, black hair. Her skin was a little darker than his and her eyes were black. Other than that, he thought she looked like him and the other kids at school. He never noticed the difference before.

"I'm not from China," Min Dee said. "My mom is part Chinese. My dad met her when he was in the army. I was born right here in the hospital. I've never lived anywhere but here. Kevin is so mean. What did he tell you to tell your mom to buy?" she asked.

"Some dinosaur shoes," answered Danny. "My mom doesn't buy things we really don't need. She says I have some good shoes. If I want dinosaur shoes I have to earn the money myself. I'm going to save the money my grandma is going to pay me."

"Is your grandma nice?" Min Dee asked.

"Yeah," Danny said. "She always treats me real nice."

They talked and walked for two more

blocks. "This is her house," Danny said as they turned up the sidewalk of a small, brick house. Danny opened the door and called, "Grandma, we're here," as they went in.

Danny loved his grandma's house. She had little knickknacks and plants on all of her shelves and tables. Danny thought she had as many plants as a greenhouse. She always had cookies and snacks for him. They went into the kitchen. Grandma stood at the sink washing a cup. "Hi, Grandma," Danny said as he put his arms around her large middle.

"Oh, Danny, I didn't hear you come in. How are you, sweetheart?" Grandma turned around. She saw Min Dee. "Well, hello there. You must be Danny's friend."

"Hi," Min Dee said shyly. "I came to help Danny."

"I'm Danny's grandma. You can call me Grandma just like Danny does. You children must be hungry. Do you want a snack? It's so nice to have so much company," Grandma said. She took a loaf of bread from the breadbox. "Do you like peanut butter and honey sandwiches?'' Grandma asked Min Dee. ''They are Danny's favorite.''

''Oh, boy. I love them,'' Min Dee said. ''They're my favorite, too.'' Danny and Min Dee smiled at each other as Grandma spread peanut butter on slices of bread.

Danny and Min Dee sat at the table. Grandma poured each of them a glass of milk. She set their sandwiches on plates in front of them. Danny hurried and took a big bite out of his sandwich. He loved the way the sticky peanut butter made the sweet honey stick to his teeth and the roof of his mouth. He washed the bite down with a gulp of milk.

''Is something wrong, Min Dee?'' Grandma asked. Danny noticed Min Dee hadn't eaten any of her sandwich. His was half gone.

''Grandma,'' Min Dee said. ''Do you have any pickles?''

''Pickles?'' Grandma said in a surprised voice.

''Pickles,'' Min Dee said with a nod. ''I like my peanut butter and honey sandwiches with dill pickles.''

40

"Well, well," Grandma said. "That's a new one on me. I think we have some dill pickle slices. I never heard of anyone eating dill pickles on peanut butter sandwiches."

Danny hadn't heard of it either. He watched as Grandma brought the jar of pickles and a fork. Min Dee opened her sandwich and covered it with green slices. She put the other slice of bread on, squashed it down and took a big bite. "Hmm, good," she said with a mouth full of sandwich. It made Danny's lips pucker to watch her take another bite. "Want to try it?" she asked him.

"Um, no thanks," he said. He didn't know how she could eat dill pickles on her peanut butter and honey sandwiches.

CHAPTER SEVEN

Invitations

Danny and Min Dee finished their sandwiches. Grandma took two small bowls from the cupboard. "Are you ready to start working?" she asked.

"What are we going to do, Grandma?" Danny asked.

"I'm going to have you help me wash leaves," Grandma told them.

"What?" Min Dee asked.

"We're going to wash the leaves on my plants," Grandma said. She poured water into each of the bowls. "The leaves

43

get dusty. The only way to dust them is to wash them."

"Why do you have to do that?" Danny asked.

Grandma handed each of them a bowl of water and some cotton balls. "They can't breathe if their faces are dirty. The plants don't get all the sun they need if their leaves are dusty. They grow better with nice, clean leaves." Grandma set a potted plant in front of each of the children. She showed them how to dip the cotton ball in the water. Then she told them how to gently and carefully wash each leaf.

"Boy, Grandma, how many plants do you have?" Min Dee asked.

"I've never counted them, dear," Grandma said.

"I bet you have hundreds," Danny guessed.

"There must be thousands and thousands of leaves," Min Dee added.

The children began washing leaves. As soon as they finished with one plant, Grandma set another one in front of them.

"Think how happy you are going to make my little friends," Grandma said.

"What?" Min Dee asked.

"Never mind me," Grandma said. "I call my plants my little friends. My little friends will be so happy to breathe nice, clean air and feel the sunshine on their bright, clean faces. This is a big help to them."

Min Dee giggled. "I never thought of having a plant for a friend before."

They finished washing the last of the leaves as it started to grow dark outside. "I better go," Min Dee said, "before it gets dark."

"Don't worry," Grandma said. "Danny and I will give you a ride home in the car. But first, I have a surprise for Danny." She took a paper sack out of the closet.

Danny opened it. He peeked inside and laughed. "Oh, wow! Thanks, Grandma," he said as he pulled out a pair of dinosaur shoes.

"Is that what you were wanting, sweetheart?" Grandma asked.

45

"Just what I wanted," Danny said. "See, they look just like Min Dee's shoes." Danny pulled off his own shoes and pulled the dinosaur shoes over his socks. "Thank you, Grandma."

"You earned them," Grandma said. "It would have taken me a month to clean all my plants if I had done them myself. Is that enough payment?"

"You bet," Danny said as he gave Grandma a big hug. "Thank you, Grandma."

"Thank you, sweetheart," Grandma said. "And for you, Min Dee, here is a little something." Grandma handed her a dollar bill. "You save it to buy something really special," Grandma told her.

"Gee, thank you, Grandma," Min Dee said.

"Come, children," Grandma said. "We better get you home."

They got their sweaters and school bags and climbed into Grandma's car. Danny and Min Dee held their feet up so they could admire their dinosaur shoes.

They took Min Dee to her house. "See you tomorrow, Danny. Bye, Grandma," she said as she slammed the car door and skipped up the sidewalk.

As they drove away, Grandma said, "What a nice friend you have, Danny."

"She is nice," Danny said. "And she is fun. She thought of a new dinosaur game to play at school. But everybody thinks she is my girlfriend. But she's not. I don't want to marry her or anything. I don't want to kiss her like Mike says I do."

"She's just your friend," Grandma said. "I think it is very nice. When I was a little girl, girls weren't friends with boys. We didn't play together. When we lined up, the girls were in one line and the boys were in another. At recess, the girls played on one side of the play-ground. The boys always played base-ball."

"Did you want to play baseball?" Danny asked.

"Yes, I did," Grandma said.

"Why didn't you?" Danny asked.

"Girls always wore dresses to school then. I didn't play baseball partly because I was wearing a dress and partly because girls just didn't play baseball with the boys. We couldn't be friends with boys like you and Min Dee can be friends."

"Was there a rule that said you couldn't?" Danny asked.

"It wasn't a rule that was written down anywhere," Grandma said. "But, it was a rule just the same because people thought that's the way it should be. I thought it was silly. But you couldn't say anything about it back then. I'm glad the rules are changing," Grandma said as she drove her car into Danny's driveway.

They went into the house. Mom was cooking supper in the kitchen. "Hi, Mom," Danny said. "Look what Grandma got for me." He pointed to his new shoes.

"Danny," Mom said with a dirty look. "Did you ask Grandma to buy those for you?"

49

"Heavens, no," Grandma interrupted. "He worked very hard to earn those shoes. I bought them while I was downtown today. Danny earned them."

"What did you do for Grandma?" Mom asked.

"Min Dee and I washed all of Grandma's plant leaves. There must have been a thousand leaves," Danny said.

"They did such a good job," Grandma added.

Mom smiled. "Very good, Danny," she said. "Would you like to stay for supper, Grandma?"

"That would be lovely," Grandma answered.

"Guess what, Mom?" Danny said. "Min Dee eats dill pickles on her peanut butter and honey sandwiches."

"Gross," Mike said as he walked into the kitchen. "Your girlfriend is weird."

"She's not my girlfriend," Danny said firmly. "She's my friend."

"And she's a very nice friend," Grandma added.

"Mike," Mother warned. "I told you to stop teasing Danny. Go wash for supper. Oh, Danny, I almost forgot. A letter came in the mail for you today."

Danny picked up an envelope off the counter. His name was printed on the front of it.

"Get a love letter?" Mike asked as he skipped out the door.

"That Mike does like to tease," Grandma said as she shook her head.

Danny opened the envelope. He pulled out an invitation. "What is it?" Mom asked.

"An invitation," Danny said. "Erica Bradley is having a birthday party. It is going to be the biggest ever. There's going to be pizza, clowns, candy, ice cream and cake, and magic tricks. Can I go? It's Friday after school. A van will pick us up and take us to Erica's house. Erica's mom and her aunt will be driving the vans."

"I suppose it will be all right," Mom said.

"But I'm not going if it's the same time as the field trip to the dinosaur dig," said Danny. "I won't miss that."

"What field trip?" asked Grandma.

"Our class might go to a dinosaur dig," said Danny. "We might get to help dig up a dinosaur. Miss Martin is going to ask the principal if our class can go."

Mike came into the kitchen. "Is your girlfriend going, too?" he asked.

He looked Mike straight in the eye. "She's just my friend," he said.

Danny took his invitation and went to wash for supper.

CHAPTER EIGHT

Just Friends

The next day, all the second grade students bubbled with excitement. Everyone had received their invitation to Erica Bradley's party. Everyone, except Kevin. At noon recess, Min Dee asked Danny, "Are you going to Erica's party Friday?"

Danny nodded. "I think everyone is."

"Kevin didn't get invited," Min Dee said. "He's really mad about it. Look, he's talking to her over by the monkey bars. Let's go see what's going on."

Danny nodded. They walked close

enough to hear what was happening. Kevin talked in a mean voice. "If you don't let me come to your party, I'm going to beat you up," he said.

Erica said, "You can boss people around on the playground, but I don't have to invite you to my party if I don't want to."

"I'll smash your face," he said as he shook his fist at her. Erica blinked and looked at the ground. "I mean it," he told her. "Tell you what," he said, "you won't have to give me any money next week if I can come to your party."

"Don't do it, Erica," Min Dee said. Kevin turned and glared at Min Dee.

"Shut up, China-woman," Kevin said.

Danny felt terrible. The look in Kevin's eyes scared him. He was afraid for Min Dee. He tugged on the back of her shirt. "Come on, Min Dee," he whispered. "Let's go play somewhere else."

Danny started to walk away. Min Dee followed him. "I don't think you should have said that," he told her.

"It's not right. How can he get away with treating people like that?" Min Dee asked. "I hope she doesn't invite him to the party."

"Me, too," Danny said. "I have a feeling there is going to be big trouble."

When recess ended, the children lined up to go into the building. While they waited, Kevin turned to Erica. "So, can I come to the party?"

"Leave her alone," Min Dee said.

"Mind your own business," Kevin told Min Dee. "Can I come, Erica?" he asked again.

Erica shrugged. "If you promise to leave me alone, you can come."

Kevin looked at Min Dee. "So there," he said. "Ha, ha, ha."

Mrs. Dummitt walked between the two lines of students in front of the doors. "There's too much talking. Be quiet," she ordered.

At the next recess, Kevin started to follow Danny and Min Dee around the playground.

"When are you getting married?" he asked. "Only sissies play with girls," he told Danny.

Danny whispered to Min Dee, "Let's stay away from him. Don't say anything to him."

The next day they tried to stay away from Kevin. It was impossible. He kept following them and teasing. At noon recess, Kevin said, "Hey, Danny, did your grandma give you some money yet?"

Danny shrugged and walked away.

"Danny," Kevin said, "bring the money your grandma gave you, I want to see it. I don't think she gave you any."

The next recess, Danny and Min Dee were playing dinosaurs in the corner of the playground. Kevin came up to them and said, "How much money did your grandma give you?"

Danny shrugged. Kevin pushed him. "Where's the money?" Kevin asked.

Danny said, "My grandma didn't give me any money."

Min Dee spoke up. "That's right, she

57

didn't. She gave him a pair of sneakers just like mine."

Kevin looked at their feet. They were wearing their matching dinosaur shoes. He started to laugh. "Are you two in love?" he teased.

Danny said, "We're just friends. There's no rule against that."

"Yeah," Min Dee added. "We're just friends. Danny's grandma gave him some sneakers. And she gave me a dollar for working for her. But we aren't going to give any of it to you, so there."

The bell rang. The other children ran to line up at the doors. Kevin shoved Min Dee. "We'll see about that," he told her as he ran toward the school.

Danny caught Min Dee's arm so she didn't fall. "You shouldn't even talk to him," he told her. "We should stay away from him. You shouldn't have told him about the dollar. It might cause trouble."

After school, Danny walked to Min Dee's house. They ate peanut butter and

honey sandwiches. Min Dee covered hers
with pickle slices.

Later, Danny went home for supper. At
the supper table, Mom said, "How was
school?"

"Stupid. Just like always," Mike said.

"How was school, Danny?" Mom
asked.

"Yesterday, Kevin made Erica invite
him to the birthday party. He said he
would smash her face if she didn't,"
Danny said.

"What?" said Mom. "Was he
teasing?"

"No, he wasn't teasing. He meant it.
And he will do it, too," Danny said.

"Is this the same boy who pushed you
the other day?" she asked.

"Yes, he's the one. He told Erica she
wouldn't have to give him any money this
week if she let him go to the party,"
Danny said.

"Why is she giving him money?"
Mom asked.

"So he'll leave her alone. Kevin wants

Min Dee to give him the dollar Grandma gave her.''

Dad and Mom both listened to Danny. ''Why doesn't the playground teacher do something to stop this?'' Mom asked.

''I tried to tell you,'' Danny said with a sigh. ''Mrs. Dummitt stands in the corner and reads a book during recess. She doesn't care. She won't do anything. If someone tells on Kevin, she says, 'Don't be a tattletale.' ''

''I think we better look into this,'' Mom said. ''It doesn't sound right to me.''

''Better hurry,'' Mike said, ''before his girlfriend gets beat up.''

''Mike, that is enough of that kind of talk,'' Mom said with a sharp voice. The telephone rang. ''Danny, please get the phone,'' Mom said.

Danny picked up the phone. A strange girl's voice said, ''Is Mike there?''

Danny smiled. ''Yeah, he's here. Who's calling, please?''

''This is Krista,'' she said.

Danny held his hand over the phone. "Oh, Mike," he said in a light voice. "It's Krista. She wants to talk to you."

Mike dropped his fork. His face turned red. "I'll talk to her in the living room," he said as he raced out of the kitchen. Danny and the rest of the family laughed. Mom said, "I don't think he will be teasing anyone about girlfriends anymore. Danny, don't you tease him."

"I won't," Danny said. "It's not nice to get teased all the time. Besides, I bet she's just a friend," he said with a laugh.

CHAPTER NINE

Trouble

When Friday came, all the second grad-ers were excited. It was the day of Erica's birthday party. Danny's mother bought a gift for her. Danny had it wrapped and tucked into his book bag.

But at noon recess, things turned ugly. Min Dee and Danny were playing dino-saurs. They raced across the playground wearing their matching dinosaur shoes. Danny said, "Min Dee, pretend I went hunting, and I got caught in the quicksand. You come looking for me and save me. Okay?''

"Okay," Min Dee said as Danny raced away to the monkey bars. He waited for her to come save him from the quicksand. She didn't come. He climbed up on the bars and looked toward the corner. Kevin was standing there. He had Min Dee trapped in the corner. Danny jumped from the top of the monkey bars and ran to help her. Min Dee tried to move around Kevin. He elbowed her in the face. Then he shoved her to the ground, jumped on top of her, grabbed her hair, and tried to rub her face in the gravel.

"Stop it!" Danny yelled as he grabbed Kevin and pulled him away from her. "Stop it!" he yelled again.

Kevin jumped to his feet and tried to slug Danny. Danny stepped aside as the fist flew past his face.

Other students quickly gathered, "Go Danny! Hit him! Get him Danny!" they yelled.

But Danny didn't hear. In his mind a

voice shouted, *Enough! Enough! Enough!*
Danny's fingers curled into a hard knot
that flew toward Kevin's face. The fist
smacked just below Kevin's eye with a
solid crack.

Suddenly, teachers came from every-
where, shouting, "Break it up! Break it
up!"

Danny was led to the principal's office.
His hand hurt. He sat by himself. It
seemed to take a long, long time. He
heard people coming and going in the outside office. He heard the bell for the after-
noon recess. Still, he sat. He wondered
what was going to happen to him.

Finally, the principal opened the office
door. Danny's mom came into the office.
"Hello, Danny," Mrs. Evans, the principal, said. "Have a seat, Mrs. Clark," she
said to Danny's mom. "Danny," the principal said, "I realize some things have
been happening that shouldn't have been.
We didn't know Kevin was causing trouble for the other students. I want you to
know there won't be any more problems

with Kevin. Students have a right to be safe when they are at school. School is supposed to be a good and happy place. Your parents and I are going to make sure that it is. Do you understand?''

Danny nodded. ''Yes,'' he said.

''Mrs. Dummitt won't be working here anymore. Monday we will have a new playground supervisor,'' the principal said. That made Danny feel good, until she said, ''But. . . .''

Danny hated that word.

''But,'' his mom said, ''it doesn't change the fact that you were fighting.''

''Fighting is against the rules,'' the principal said. ''You will have to be punished for fighting. You will have to stay after school tonight.''

''Tonight?'' Danny exclaimed. ''Tonight is the birthday party.''

''I'm sorry, Danny,'' Mom said. ''I think it is best. It was wrong to hit that boy.''

''It isn't fair,'' Danny said. ''Kevin started it.''

"Kevin will be punished, too," the principal said. "You won't have to worry about him causing trouble anymore. We will make sure of that. School is almost over for today. You stay and sit on the bench in the outside office for a half-hour more. Then it will all be over and we can forget all of this. Okay?"

Danny nodded. He went to sit in the outside office. His mom left to go home as the dismissal bell rang for the other students. "I'll see you at home," she said as she walked out of the office. Danny was glad Kevin wouldn't be able to hurt anyone anymore. But he really wanted to go to the party. It was going to be the biggest and best birthday party ever, and he wouldn't be there. He tried very hard not to cry. He thought about one good thing. At least he wouldn't have to miss the trip to the dinosaur dig. If he had to miss something, he'd rather miss the birthday party. He wondered when they would find out if they could go. Miss Martin said it might be a couple of weeks

67

before they knew. The class would just have to be patient. Danny didn't like to be patient. It sure seemed to take a long time.

CHAPTER TEN

Dinosaurs for Lunch

A half-hour could sure go slow. Danny watched the big clock in the office. The minutes seemed to drag. At first he hoped the others would wait for him to go to the party. Watching out the window, he saw two shiny vans park in front of the school. Danny watched as his classmates, one at a time, gathered around and started to climb aboard.

Danny couldn't stand to look. He turned around on the bench so he didn't have to. He propped his elbows on his knees and leaned his head on his arms. Danny stared at the floor. The school grew quiet, except for the steady clack of the secretary's typewriter. Danny thought about all the things that had happened. Sometimes it seemed like things were very unfair. Sometimes it was hard to know the rules. What were good rules? What were just silly ideas everyone thought were rules?

He knew the rule that said, *Don't Fight,* was a good rule. It kept people from getting hurt. But the things Kevin did were against the rules. Kevin tried to hurt people. He got away with it because Mrs. Dummitt didn't mind the rules. She shouldn't have been reading when she was supposed to be watching the playground. Rules work when everyone keeps them, Danny thought with a sad sigh.

The rule that said, *You Can't Have A Girl For A Friend,* is just a silly idea, he decided. It doesn't hurt anyone. I like Min Dee. She thinks of good games. I like to play with her. I like her even if she eats pickles on her peanut butter and honey sandwiches.

Then Danny thought about Min Dee. He hoped she was having a good time at the party. At least she could tell him if it really was the biggest, best birthday party ever. Maybe she'll bring me some candy, he hoped.

"Danny?" A quiet voice interrupted his thoughts. "You can go now," the school secretary said with a smile. "Your time is up. You can go home now."

Danny walked up the empty hall. He took his sweater and book bag from his coat hook on the wall by his classroom.

As he stepped outside onto the playground, a voice said, "It's about time."

Danny turned. "Min Dee, what are you doing?" he asked.

She leaned against the building. "I'm waiting for you," she said with a smile.

"Why aren't you at the party?" Danny asked.

She shrugged. "I didn't feel like going.

71

It wouldn't be any fun if you weren't there. Want to come to my house to play?"

"But they're having clowns and cake and candy at the party," Danny said.

Min Dee pulled a dollar out of her pocket. "We can stop at the store and buy some candy. Your Grandma said to buy something special with it. I'll buy you a candy bar. Besides, when we get to my house, we can make some peanut butter and honey sandwiches. I like them better than I like cake and ice cream anyway," she said.

"So do I," Danny said.

"Hey, Danny, did you hear Kevin got kicked out of school? He can't come back for a week or more. His mother had to come get him and his books and make-up work. I hope he gets into trouble. The teachers said there won't be any more trouble on the playground."

"I know," Danny said. "We're supposed to have a new playground teacher. That'll be a good thing."

"Danny?" Min Dee said softly as they walked down the sidewalk together. "Thank you for what you did for me today."

"It was nothing," Danny said. "I didn't want Kevin to hurt you."

"You're the best friend ever," she said.

"Min Dee? Do you have some pickles at your house?" Danny asked.

"We have lots and lots. We have a whole jar of pickles."

"I might try one, just one, bite of a peanut butter, honey, and pickle sandwich," Danny said.

Min Dee smiled. Danny smiled. He'd try it. He knew there was no rule that said he had to like it.

Danny tipped his head backward. He gave a giant roar. Min Dee laughed and roared too. They walked down the street roaring at each other like a couple of wild dinosaurs.